Disney
5-Minute
PRINCESS
Stories

Written by Liza Baker
Illustrated by Robbin Cuddy

Disney
PRESS

New York

Printed in the United States of America

ISBN 0-7868-3300-9

Library of Congress Catalog Card Number: 2001088828

Visit www.disneybooks.com

Contents

Beauty and the Beast

The Sleigh Ride

Long ago, an enchantress cast a spell on a castle. She transformed the handsome young prince into a hideous beast and his servants into household objects.

"Just look at me," grumbled the Beast. "I've been so cruel, holding Belle captive in my castle. How will she ever see me as anything but a monster?"

"Come now," said Mrs. Potts gently. "All you have to do is show her what is inside your heart."

"You must act like a gentleman!" Lumiere the candelabrum chimed in. "Be romantic. Compliment her. And most of all, be kind, gentle, and sincere!"

"And don't be so grumpy!" added Chip, Mrs. Potts's young son.

Mrs. Potts gave her son a stern look. But they all knew Chip was right.

"I have an idea!" said the Beast, smiling. "Why don't I invite Belle to go on a sleigh ride? It just snowed outside, and she might like the fresh air."

"Perfect!" said Lumiere.

"A wonderful idea," agreed Mrs. Potts.

"Very romantic," added Chip.

"That's enough out of you," Mrs. Potts said to Chip, trying not to smirk.

The Beast sent Lumiere to extend his invitation.

"That sounds lovely!" said Belle. "I've been stuck in this castle far too long."

Belle ran down the long staircase and stepped outside. Glimmering white snowflakes fell from the sky. It was a perfect winter day.

Just then, the Beast pulled up in a gleaming horse-drawn sleigh.

"How beautiful!" exclaimed Belle.

The Beast smiled as he took her hand and helped her into the sleigh. He didn't mention that he had spent all morning polishing it just for her. Once she was settled, he covered her with a warm blanket.

They took off across the powdery snow. Belle laughed happily as
the Beast guided the sleigh through the forest path. Soon they
came to a clearing in the woods. Before them was a frozen pond.
The Beast pulled on the reins and stopped at the edge of the pond.

"This is such a magical place," said Belle. "How did you ever find it?"

"I used to come here long ago," said the Beast. "It was one of my favorite places. I wanted to . . . um . . . share it with you."

Then the Beast took out a picnic basket filled with hot chocolate, cookies, bread, and fruit.

When they had finished their meal, the Beast asked Belle if she wanted to ice-skate.

"Oh, yes," she replied. "Father and I used to go every winter. I love ice-skating!"

Soon Belle was spinning effortlessly across the pond's smooth surface. The Beast was less graceful. Hitting a bump in the ice, he lost his balance and toppled to the ground. At first he was angry, but then he saw Belle looking at him kindly. Remembering his friends' advice, he smiled as Belle helped him to his feet.

"Everyone falls sometimes," said Belle. "It's part of learning."

Before long, they were gliding across the ice arm in arm, enjoying each other's company in the crisp winter air.

They grew tired and decided to rest. Just then, a timid fawn wandered out of the forest.

"Poor thing," said Belle. "She looks scared and hungry." Taking an apple from their picnic basket, Belle showed the Beast how to gently feed the young deer.

Soon the sun was setting. It was time to go. As they made their way home, Belle thought about the day she had spent with the Beast. There was something different about him. He had shown Belle a kinder, softer side. Perhaps they could be friends, after all. . . .

Cinderella

The Dance Lesson

"Just imagine," said Cinderella excitedly. "There's a ball at the palace tonight in honor of the Prince. And every maiden in the land is invited. That means me, too!"

All of Cinderella's friends clapped and chirped as they gathered around. They loved their "Cinderelly."

"Oh, dear," said Cinderella with a sigh. "There is so much to do! I can only go if I finish my chores. And today, Stepmother has given me more work than ever. There is washing, mending, ironing, cooking, scrubbing, sweeping, and . . ."

Suddenly three loud shrieks came from downstairs.

"Cinderellllllaaaa! Come down here immediately, and help us get ready for the ball!" her stepsisters cried together.

Her cruel stepmother and stepsisters wouldn't give poor Cinderella any time to do the rest of her chores.

"Mend my dress!" screeched Anastasia.

"Polish my shoes!" whined Drizella.

"Iron my cloak!" demanded her stepmother.

Hours later, Cinderella began to sweep and scrub the endless stone floor.

Suddenly Jaq had an idea. "I know!" he said. "We help-a, Cinderelly!"

All of the other mice nodded in agreement.

"What would I do without you!" said Cinderella, patting them each on the head. "You are so good to me."

Everyone joined in the cleaning, singing happily as they went.

As she worked, Cinderella began to imagine the magical evening ahead. Everyone would be dressed in the finest clothes. Cinderella would wear her mother's beautiful gown. The ballroom would come alive with music, dancing, and laughter. The handsome young Prince would bow before Cinderella and ask her to dance.

Suddenly Cinderella stopped dreaming.

"Oh, no!" she cried. "I've never been to a ball. I don't even know how to dance!"

"Don't you worry, Cinderelly!" Jaq smiled reassuringly. "Us show you dance! Easy pie!"

With that, Jaq bowed before Perla and extended his hand. "Dance, please, missy?" he asked.

Perla blushed as she took Jaq's hand.

Gus was the conductor. He got all the birds to sing.

Jaq and Perla spun around and around, gliding across the floor.

Cinderella watched and then copied their movements.

"Just listen and move! See?" said Perla. "Not so scary."

Using her broom as an imaginary partner, Cinderella danced and twirled gracefully throughout the room. She led everyone across the floor, sweeping and cleaning as they went.

"Good-good, Cinderelly!" said Jaq, beaming. "Lucky Prince gets to dance with Cinderelly."

The mice collapsed on the floor, laughing.

"Thank you all so much," Cinderella told her friends. "With your help, tonight might be the night that all my dreams come true!"

THE LITTLE MERMAID

A Special Surprise

The underwater kingdom was quiet and peaceful. Every mermaid and merman was in bed fast asleep—everyone but Princess Ariel and her friend Flounder.

"Hurry up, Flounder!" cried Ariel. "It's almost time for the party. We can't be late!"

Trying not to make a sound, Ariel and Flounder swam away from King Triton's palace. They began their journey toward the surface.

"B-b-but, Ariel," said Flounder, "are you sure we should go to the surface? Remember the last time? Your father got so angry. You know how he feels about humans!"

"That's why this time, we can't get caught!" said Ariel, smiling. She wasn't going to let anything ruin her plans for tonight.

Prince Eric, the prince Ariel had saved in a shipwreck, was having a royal ball. Ariel had a very special surprise for him.

"Swim faster, Flounder!" she cried, glancing back at him. Flounder raced to keep up.

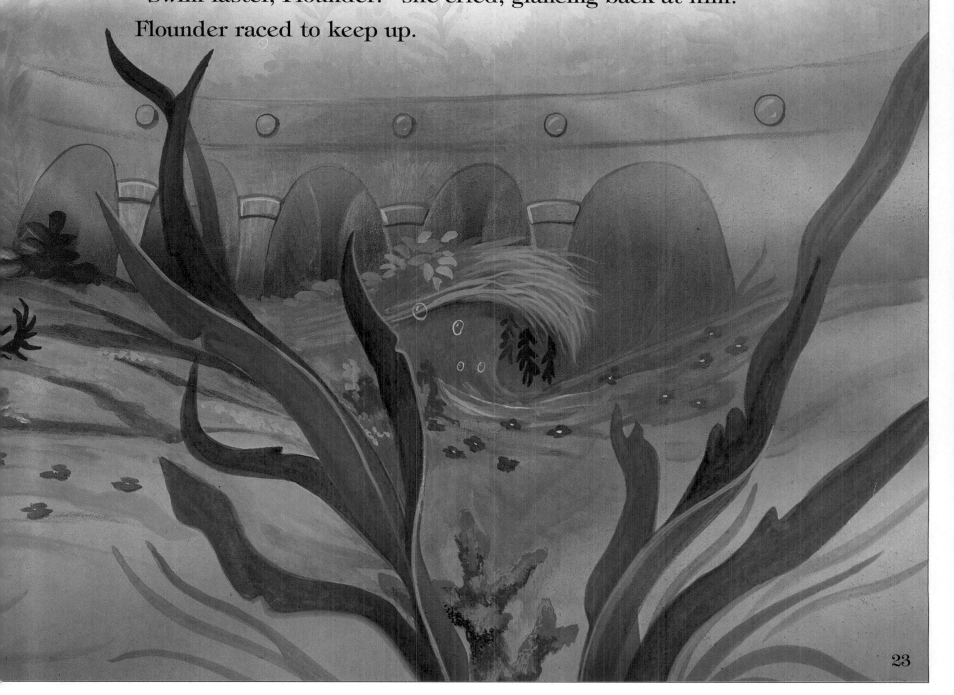

Just as Ariel and Flounder approached the surface, Ariel saw
beautiful lights dance across the water. When they poked their
heads out of the water, Ariel and Flounder saw colorful lights
explode in the air above Prince Eric's castle.

"I've never seen anything so beautiful in all my life," said Ariel
breathlessly. "The human world is a wonderful place!"

"It sure is pretty!" said Flounder.

Off in the distance, Prince Eric stood on the palace balcony. He just didn't feel like joining in the royal celebration. He couldn't stop thinking about the mysterious girl with the lovely voice who had saved his life in the shipwreck. Why has she disappeared? he wondered.

Flounder spotted the prince first.

"Look, Ariel," he said, pointing a fin at the castle.

Ariel's heart leaped with joy when she saw Prince Eric.

"It's time for my surprise!" she said, winking at Flounder.

Swimming up to a nearby rock, Ariel and Flounder hid behind it.

"R-r-ready?" asked Flounder.

With a nod, Ariel closed her eyes, opened her mouth, and began to sing.

Suddenly, the night was filled with the sweet sound of Ariel's voice. She sang a song she had written just for Eric. It was Ariel's special gift to him.

Hearing her beautiful voice again, Eric's face lit up. "It can't be!" he said. "I must be hearing the sounds of the wind." Still, he remained on the balcony, enchanted by the beautiful song filling the night air.

When the song was over, Eric looked out across the sea. He hoped to catch a glimpse of the wonderful girl who had saved him.

"Who are you?" he called out into the night. But all he heard was the echo of his own voice.

"I'll be back soon," Ariel whispered as she and Flounder swam toward home. "Just wait and see. . . ."

Snow White
and the Seven Dwarfs

A Friend in Need

"Whatever could be keeping the Seven Dwarfs?" said Snow White. "It's getting late. They should have been home from the diamond mine by now!"

While she waited, Snow White busied herself tidying up their cottage in the woods. "What messy little fellows!" she said.

Just then, Happy came through the front door. He tugged on Snow White's long yellow skirt.

"Snow White," he said. "Come quickly! A young deer is hurt in the woods."

"Oh, no!" cried Snow White. "The poor thing! We must hurry!"

They soon reached a small clearing. Everyone stood in a circle around the deer.

"Thank goodness you're here, Snow White!" said Doc. "This little fella's in trouble!"

"He must be cold," said Snow White, covering him with her long cape.

"Maybe he's just tired," said Sleepy, yawning. "A nice long rest should do the trick!"

"Why, you could be right, Sleepy," said Snow White. "But he's not closing his eyes, so I think it might be something else."

"Maybe he has a . . . aaahhhhh . . . aaahhhhhhh . . . chooooooooo . . . a cold," said Sneezy. "He looks like he might feel a bit stuffy."

"Well, that's possible. But then he probably would have stayed in his thicket until he was feeling better," said Snow White.

"I know!" said Happy. "Maybe he's feeling sad and needs a little cheering up!"

"I'm sure that would help, Happy," said Snow White. "But he looks like he may need something more than a merry story or a song."

"I, uh . . . don't know for sure," said Bashful softly. "But perhaps he's too shy to let us know what's the matter."

"We all feel shy sometimes, don't we, Bashful?" said Snow White.

Then Dopey started pacing back and forth and pointing over his shoulder.

"Hmm," said Snow White. "You could be right, Dopey. He could be lost."

"I'll bet I know what happened," grumbled Grumpy. "The wicked Queen probably cast a spell on him! She's always up to no good!"

Suddenly, Doc pushed his way past the others and approached the deer. "May I lake a took—er, I mean, take a look?" he asked, adjusting his eyeglasses.

Doc knelt down beside the deer.

"Well, would you look at that!" cried Doc. "The poor deer must have stepped on a thorn. Ouch!"

Doc gently removed the sharp thorn. The deer jumped up and licked him.

"Oh, how relieved you must be!" cried Snow White. "Now run along home," she said to their new friend. "Your family must be worried about you!"

The deer licked Snow White's hand and ran off into the forest.

Snow White and the Seven Dwarfs went home to their little cottage.

"I am so proud of each and every one of you," said Snow White, smiling at her friends. "You each did your best to help a friend in need!"

That night, Snow White and the Seven Dwarfs made a delicious dinner. Then when they'd all eaten their fill, they sang and danced until it was time for bed.

Aladdin

The Mysterious Voyage

Aladdin and Jasmine had just gotten married. People had come from near and far to celebrate. It had been the largest wedding in the history of Agrabah!

Now Aladdin and Jasmine were preparing to take a romantic trip far, far away.

"Abu, stay out of those bags!" warned Aladdin, smiling at his curious little friend. "That food is for our trip!

"Jasmine is going to be so surprised when she sees what I've planned!" said Aladdin as he finished packing. "She has lived most of her life within the walls of this palace. Now we're going to see the world . . . together!"

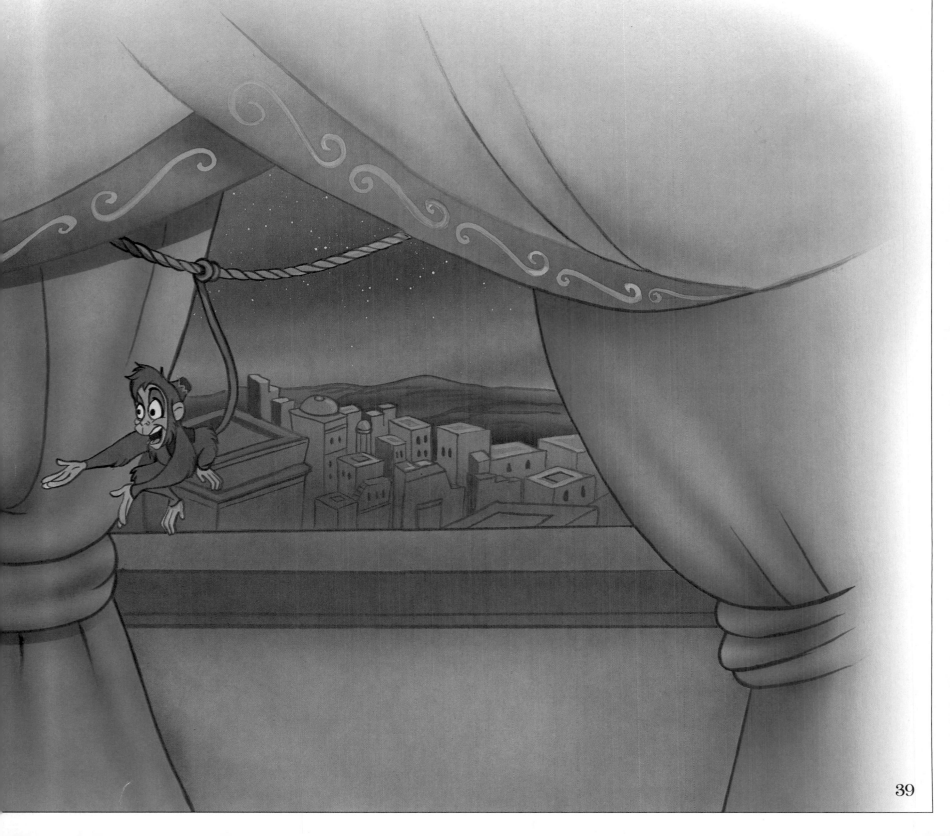

Soon Aladdin and Jasmine stood on the balcony, ready to begin their adventure.

"Madame, the Magic Carpet awaits you," said Aladdin, bowing before his new bride.

"Won't you tell me where we're going?" Jasmine asked as she took his hand. "I'm dying of curiosity."

"You are going to see things you've never ever seen before—a whole new, exciting world," Aladdin replied.

"Let's get going," said Jasmine. "I can't wait!"

Jasmine, Aladdin, and Abu settled onto the Magic Carpet. Then they took off, soaring high above the palace. Jasmine laughed with delight, the wind blowing her long hair behind her.

"Look how small everything looks!" she said. "It's like a dream."

After a little while, the Magic Carpet began its descent. "Are we there?" asked Jasmine.

"Almost," said Aladdin. "Close your eyes. I want this to be a surprise." Jasmine closed her eyes.

"No peeking!" Aladdin said.

Suddenly, the Magic Carpet landed on top of a high cliff. Jasmine heard a loud noise that sounded like crashing water.

"Can I open my eyes?" she asked excitedly.

"Okay. Open, sesame!" said Aladdin. "This, Jasmine, is the ocean!"

Jasmine couldn't believe her eyes. She had never ever seen anything so beautiful! The water was a brilliant shade of turquoise. Dolphins leaped in and out of the water as if they were dancing. Huge ocean waves crashed onto a white sandy beach in the distance.

"This *is* another world!" said Jasmine, her eyes shining happily. "I've read about the ocean, but I can't believe I'm actually seeing it with my own eyes. It's magical!"

They had a wonderful time swimming and enjoying the sun. When he and Jasmine were ready to go, Aladdin snapped his fingers. "Time for our next destination!" he said.

Within seconds, the Magic Carpet appeared. "I don't suppose you'll tell me what you've planned next," said Jasmine.

"That would ruin the surprise!" said Aladdin. "But I promise it will give you the chills."

Once again, Aladdin asked Jasmine to cover her eyes. As they descended, Jasmine felt the air grow colder. Suddenly she felt a warm coat hugging her shoulders.

"Okay, Jasmine," said Aladdin excitedly. "You can open your eyes now!"

This time, everywhere that Jasmine looked, she saw white!

"Oh . . . what is it?" she asked, bending down to touch the cold white powder.

"It's snow!" answered Aladdin. "Isn't it wonderful? It falls from the sky when it's cold."

"It's amazing!" cried Jasmine. "It looks like a soft white cloud!

"Watch out!" she cried. Abu had thrown a snowball. It was heading straight for Aladdin.

They spent the rest of the day playing in the snow. They built snowmen and made snow angels. They even used the Magic Carpet as a sled to slide down a nearby hill over and over again.

Soon the sun began to set, and the air grew even colder.

"I think it's time to go!" said Aladdin. They climbed onto the Magic Carpet and took off.

"You've shown me places so different from Agrabah," said Jasmine happily. "There are plenty of brand-new worlds for us to share."

As they made their way back to the palace, Jasmine smiled. She knew that this was just the beginning of their wonderful life together.